The BEARS' AUTUMN

by Keizaburo Tejima

translated from the Japanese
by Susan Matsui

A Star & Elephant Book
The Green Tiger Press
La Jolla
1986

The autumn mountains of Hokkaido, the northern island of Japan, are aflame with beautiful colors. The clear sky seems to spread out forever.

The chilly autumn wind comes blowing, and a jay calls.

Something dark is moving about in the forest. There's a little one, too. It's a mother and baby brown bear. They're eating something to fatten up for their long winter sleep.

Mother and Baby Bear are eating tasty, ripe wild grapes.

Baby Bear with his light body
is a better tree-climber than
his mother.

"I wonder what I can see
from the top of this tree."

From high up in the tree, Baby Bear sees sparkling white mountains in the distance. And he sees a beautiful river.

"I'm going to fish for salmon in that river tonight," thinks Baby Bear excitedly. It would be his very first trip to fish for salmon.

When the sunset fades and moonlight shines on the forest, Mother and Baby Bear come to the edge of the river.

"Will they come? Will they really come?" asks Baby Bear.

"Yes, of course they will."

"Oh, here they come!"

Sparkling white shadows appear one after another, coming up the river.

It is a school of salmon.
Mother Bear gets ready to jump.

Mother Bear disappears beneath the water. When she comes up again, she is holding a big salmon in her mouth.

Baby Bear comes swimming excitedly, but Mother Bear says,
"Go catch one for yourself."

Baby Bear chases the salmon as fast as he can. But try as he might, he can't catch them.

"That's it. I'll try diving as Mommy did."

It is a strange world beneath the water, wavering and sparkling blue in the moonlight.

Baby Bear can come close to the salmon, and they won't
swim away.

He's got it!

Baby Bear climbs out of the river, proudly holding a fine, big salmon in his mouth. He shakes himself all over.

Baby Bear eats salmon for the first time in his life.
How good it tastes, the salmon he has caught all by himself!

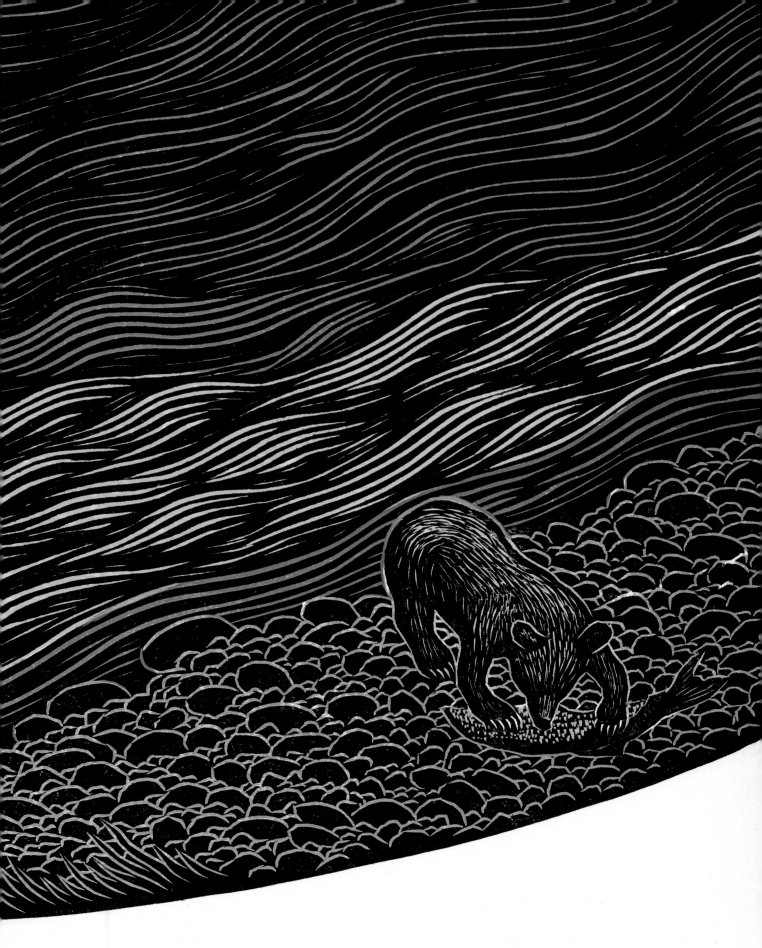

On the river behind him, the moonlight sparkles and swirls,

and becomes a big, big fish.

The lively little bear decides to catch it.

"Mommy, look! There's a great big fish in here!"

"Silly little bear, that's just the moonlight on the water!" Mother Bear says, with a gentle smile.

When the moon has set and the night sky is full of stars,
Baby Bear is back in the den, sleeping by his mother's side.

He has a dream about a big, big fish. Twinkling like the stars, the fish swims slowly through the night sky.

Text and illustrations copyright © 1986 by Keizaburo Tejima
First published by Fukutake Publishing Co., Ltd., Tokyo, Japan.
American edition copyright © 1986 by The Green Tiger Press, La Jolla, California.
ISBN: 0-88138-080-6
Library of Congress Catalog Card Number 86-81315
First Edition • Third Printing

The illustrations are reproduced from original woodcuts.
The text is set in Albertus Book
by Professional Typography, San Diego, California.
Printed and bound in Hong Kong.